A Parcel of Pigs and other Funny 'tails'

Poems and pictures by Andréa Prior

Matador
9 Priory Business Park,
Wistow Road, Kibworth Beauchamp,
Leicestershire. LE8 0RX
Tel: 0116 279 2299
Email: books@troubador.co.uk
Web: www.troubador.co.uk/matador
Twitter: @matadorbooks

ISBN 978 1785898 907

British Library Cataloguing in Publication Data.
A catalogue record for this book is available from the British Library.

Printed and bound by CPI Group (UK) Ltd, Croydon, CR0 4YY
Typeset in 19pt Book Anitqua by Troubador Publishing Ltd, Leicester, UK

Matador is an imprint of Troubador Publishing Ltd

This book is dedicated to...
My wonderful parents Eve and Bill, who showed me love,
laughter and bundles of fun, and I thank you both for reading
to me endlessly when I was very young.

This book belongs to

_____

Acknowledgements

I would like to thank my friends and family who provided help and support during the writing and illustrating of this book, and to those of you who took the time to read, listen and offer comments.

A special thanks to my dear friend Martin Smart, who has not only worked with me on the design of this book but who has been an inspiration to me throughout my career.

Last but never least my darling husband JP who encouraged me to "Get on with it!"

Before we begin…

I love the musicality of rhyme and my ideas come from anywhere and everywhere; people I love, people I don't, friends I talk to, stories they tell, countries I visit, things I see, things I do, phrases I hear, dreams I dream.

When I was young, my mother read to me every night and I look back at those times as truly magical. Rhymes we read together were my favourites and I was inspired by the work of A. A. Milne, Roald Dahl and the nonsense poems of Edward Lear.

There is something enchanting about rhyme; not only is it great to read aloud but it is also an ideal way to help children with their reading and linguistic development. It helps with spelling, pronunciation, and memory recall and lets them have fun with language. It helps children to understand word patterns, words that share common sounds and to read with energy and liveness, which will be so important to them in later life.

I love writing rhymes; they make learning fun, and my poems are written for those parents and children that love reading together!

Go on!
Open the parcel and see What's inside!
Have FUN!!

Contents

Silly Ducks

Ducks a' talking *quack, quack, quack,*
Ducks a' walking *clack, clack, clack,*
That side – this side – which side – your side,
Can't keep up with the *quack, clack, quacks!*

Ducks a' swimming *paddle, paddle, paddle,*
Ducks a' strolling *waddle, waddle, waddle,*
This side – that side – which side – your side,
Can't keep up with the *waddle, paddle, waddles!*

Shall we talk about this poem?

How many times can you say 'QUACK, CLACK, QUACKS' and
'WADDLE, PADDLE, WADDLES' without getting tongue-tied?

Why not give each duck a name?

Why are they good names for the ducks?

Cecilia's Mother

Cecilia's mother is as MAD as a hare,
With a huge big mouth and a wide eyed stare,
She barks and shouts and snorts and sprouts,
Hairs from her nose and rings on her toes,
"Get out!" She cries, she cries, cries she,
She's the scariest mother I've ever seen!

Cecilia's mother is as TALL as a tree,
With legs so long they're taller than me!
Her beads and pearls she twists and twirls,
With her big red hair and her frightening glare,
"Buzz off!" She cries, she cries, cries she,
She's the spookiest mother I've ever seen!

Shall we talk about this poem?

What scares you the most about Cecilia's mother?

Make up your own scary story about what she might do!

Would it scare you?

PORKER POST

HANDLE WITH CARE
AND KINDNESS

6

A Parcel of Pigs

A parcel of pigs and a gaggle of geese,
A mountain of mice with a chunk of cheese,
"What's that?" said the pigs to the mice with the cheese,
"It's none of your business Mr Pig if you please!"

A pen of hens and a bumble of bees,
A warbling sparrow with two knocking knees,
"How's that?" said the hens to the sparrow with the knees,
"Well never you mind Mrs Hen if you please!"

A cauldron of cats with some sleepy old fleas,
A bundle of bats fast asleep in the trees,
"Wake up!" said the cats to the bats and the fleas,
"Please do be quiet Mrs Cat if you please!"

A haram of hares and a tumble of trees,
A rumble of rabbits with a golden key,
"What's that?" said the hares to the rabbits with the key,
"Mind your own beeswax Mr Hare if you please!"

Shall we talk about this poem?
How many eyes can you count in the picture?
If you had a pet pig, what would you call it?
Why?

7

Where is Everybody?

Humphrey the hippo was VERY upset,
His brother went missing on a trip to the vet,
He'd lost his mother the day before,
And his father went missing in the local store,
His sister had vanished whilst walking the cat,
It was all a dilemma and that was that!

Humphrey shouted and yelled and hollered and bawled,
"WHERE ARE YOU ALL?!" he called and called;
**"Oh sister, brother, father, mother,
WHERE ARE YOU ALL?!"** he called.

But then….

His brother appeared from behind the flowers,
His mother turned up after hours and hours,
His father came back with the shopping at last,
His sister came back with the cat and asked…

"Oh Humphrey, Oh Humphrey,
Why look that way at me?
You silly old hippo!
We're ALWAYS back for tea!"

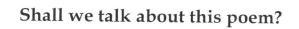

Shall we talk about this poem?

Whom had Humphrey lost?

Who came back with the cat?

What tasty teatime treats do you think the Hippo family like?

9

Jolly Mr Toad

Mr Toad lives at the end of the road,
Very jolly is he, very jolly indeed.

Mr Mouse lives at the top of the house,
Very happy is he, very happy indeed.

But Mrs Hen lives in a very small pen,
Very sad is she, very sad indeed.

Mrs Cat lives on a small comfy mat,
Very cosy is she, very cosy indeed.

But Mr Bird thinks this is all quite absurd,
Very chirpy is he, very chirpy indeed.

Shall we talk about this poem?

Where does Mrs Cat live?

How far might it be from the toad pond?

Who else do you think lives in the pond?

Nosh-nosh!

I can't stop eating I'm getting so tubby,
I'm about to burst I'm looking so chubby,
I can't stop munching it's all so yummy!

Gobble-gobble,
wolf-wolf,
guzzle-guzzle, gulp!
Nosh-nosh, nibble-nibble, gobble-gobble,
WOLF!

Shall we talk about this poem?

How many things you can see on the table?

What is your favourite flavour ice cream?

How many times can you say

'Nosh- nosh, nibble-nibble, gobble-gobble, WOLF!

Mustard Mike

Michael has a mustard jumper
That his mother makes him wear,
It's such a funny colour,
That people stop and stare!

It's accompanied by trousers
In a funny shade of purple,
Such a weird combination
That he's looking like a turtle!

Michael has a mustard jumper
That he seems to wear each day,
And with his funny purple trousers
He's going to pass my way!

What should I say?
What can I do?

I think I'll run and hide like you!

Shall we talk about this poem?

How many children are hiding from Mustard Mike?

Do you have a favourite jumper?

What colour is it?

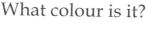

Nosy Parker

Parker is my *purr*-fect pet,
My pussycat my *purr*-fect friend,
He's round and fluffy, ginger and puffy
With big green eyes, he's worldly-wise.

Full of mischief catching mice,
Very naughty but very nice,
He keeps me safe with lots of hugs,
He chases birds and chases bugs.

My sister came to stay one day,
When I had gone on holiday,
The cat he found a tiny mouse
That ran and ran around the house.

The mouse it ran right up the stairs,
My sister followed everywhere,
The cat he tried to catch the mouse
In every corner of the house!

But Mr. Mouse was far too speedy,
And was getting rather greedy,
He started eating Parker's food
But Parker, he was not amused!
He knocked the mouse right off his dish,
"GET OFF; GET OUT MY BOWL OF FISH!

The mouse he ran right out the door,
My sister slipped upon the floor,
So Parker followed close behind,
The mouse he went to try and find,
But crafty mouse had got away
And lived to fight another day.

Shall we talk about this poem?

Why is Parker cross with the crafty mouse?

Do you have a cat?

Make up a story about your cat chasing a mouse.

I'm an Onion

I'm an onion,
Round and red,
I have a thick skin
And it covers my head.

I'm good in stews,
Well that's good news!
I'm even better in a tart,
The really tasty part.

I make a good salad,
And with quiche I'm a ballad…
…of flavours, all tasty and strong,
But a casserole dish is where I belong.

I'm an onion,
In a pan with its lid,
However you eat me,
You'll be glad that you did.

Shall we talk about this poem?

What are the names of Papa Onion's friends?

Who is your favourite onion?

What food do you eat that has onions in it?

My Sleepless Night

It's 4am and I'm wide-awake,
It's 4am and my tummy aches,
The moon is bright
It's the middle of the night,
Why CAN'T I go to sleep!

I count some sheep but still can't sleep,
I read my book but have no luck,
I'm STILL awake and it's half past four
So I get my book and read some more,
Why CAN'T I go to sleep!

It's 5am and I'm still awake!
What MUST I do, what WILL it take
To send me off to sleep again,
I count more sheep and count to ten,
Why CAN'T I go to sleep!

It's 7am and my eyes are shut,
At last, at last I've gone to sleep…BUT;
The alarm clock goes RING-RING! RING-RING!
My mobile goes PING-PING! PING-PING!
"It's time to rise," the clock it cries!
But I just want to go to sleep!

Shall we talk about this poem?
What is on the cover of the book the boy is reading?
What books do you like to read when you go to bed?
What do <u>you</u> do when you can't sleep?

Silly Dirty Monkey

Silly dirty monkey,
Hasn't washed for years,
He's matted and he's tatted,
But I don't think he cares!

Silly dirty monkey,
Never keeping clean,
He's smelly and he's filthy,
In fact, he's quite obscene!

You SILLY dirty monkey,
Why don't you have a wash?
You'll smell and feel delightful,
In fact, you'll look quite posh!

Shall we talk about this poem?

Which hand is Silly Dirty Monkey using to swing from the tree?

Are you a Silly Monkey?

What's the naughtiest thing you have done?

"Barnaby was Bothered"

Barnaby was bothered
As he couldn't find his hat,
He'd left it on the garden gate
And that he thought was that.
But when he went to find it,
The hat had disappeared,
He couldn't find it anywhere
And that he thought was weird.

So he searched his room and under his bed,
He glanced inside the garden shed,
He peered on shelves and under the stairs,
Under the table and under the chairs,
Under the sofa and under the carpet,
He even looked in the village market!
He looked in the garden and found nothing there,
He looked in the cupboards and they were all bare!

He began to shout and cry in gloom,
"I've looked and looked in every room,
Where must I look to find my hat?
I'm very bothered and that is that! "

Shall we talk about this poem?

In how many places does Barnaby look for his hat?

Can you name all of the places?

How many hats do you have and what colours are they?

Bumble-ena

Bumble-ena is a VERY smart bee,
A VERY smart bee is she.

She flies so high
In the bright blue sky,
She dives to the left
And dips to the right,
She climbs and soars
In the beautiful light.

She tumbles and swoops
In great big hoops,
She plunges and falls
And buzzes and calls,
Her friends they follow
At the side of the swallows.

They plummet and lunge
And dip and plunge,
All day long.

Shall we talk about this poem?

What is Bumble-ena wearing on her head?

How many stripes does Bumble-ena have?

What sound does a bee make when it flies?

Shall we talk about this poem?

How many of Professor Prior's puppets can you find?

Can you find 10 words beginning with 'P' in the poem?

What song do you think they are singing?

Professor Prior's Puppet Choir

In the Puppet choir of Professor Prior
Performed a pink pig and a very tall friar,
A podgy pop-eyed pastry cook,
Eating a pear and reading a book.

A perfect purple pearl piano
Played by plump Miss Patsy Parrow,
Mr. Parrow with his potent drink,
Passionately singing with cheeks so pink.

Powerful wails of three striped cats
Looking perfectly prudish in three peaked hats,
Precariously perched were a parrot and crow
Practising poetry, 'Rock to and rock fro.'

But the pint-sized man in the pin-striped suit
Only puffed on his pipe and picked at his foot.
The peculiar pupils of Professor Prior,
When told not to persist,
They only sang
HIGHER!

Go Fetch!

"**Go fetch**!" said the man to the dog with the bone,
"**No I will not**!" said the dog with a groan,
"'I'm perfectly happy here with my bone,
So you **GO FETCH** and leave me alone!"

Shall we talk about this poem?

What colour is the ball in the picture?

Do you have a pet dog?

What does your dog chase as well as a ball?

Eddie's New Pet

When Eddie was ten, just now and again
He would ask for a tiger to be his best friend.

"Tigers are tough and they're terribly rough,"
His father would try to explain,
But Eddie was certain and pulled back the curtain
To show his new pet on a chain.

His pet he called Nigel, not Timmy or Simon,
'Cos Nigel's a cracking good name,
He thought about Wayne or Billy or Shane,
But they were just all rather plain.

So Nigel and Eddie went out for spaghetti
At the local Italian bar,
The guests were amazed and totally dazed,
And some they ran out to their car.

Eddie tried to explain, "Nigel's friendly and tame,
He's my pet and he's terribly shy!"
Nigel let out a roar and flicked out his claw,
And the guests they all ran for the door.

"We'd better go home," Eddie said with a groan,
And Nigel he had to agree.
So they asked for the bill and ran down the hill,
And went for a swim in the sea.

Shall we talk about this poem?
Where would you take Nigel the tiger if he were your pet?
What animal would you like for your best friend?
Why?

33

THe ENd

About the Author

Andréa Prior is a writer and illustrator who lives between the South Downs of England and the South West of Spain with her husband John.

She has a degree in illustration from Leeds University and spent her formative career working as an illustrator and Artist's Agent in children's publishing. She has also had several successful art exhibitions before pursuing a rewarding and thriving business career in the branding and design industry at director level.

Andréa grew up in a safari park near Durham, where as a child she worked as a Park Ranger in 'Pet's Corner', looking after llamas, goats, monkeys, pot-bellied pigs and a lion cub! Her love of animals, passion for illustration and writing children's verse has inspired this book of rhyming poems.

Andréa is also an accomplished classical pianist and loves teaching children of all ages to develop their love of music.